JUST PLAYING

by Anita Wadley Schlaht

illustrated by Hazel Conley

ISBN 978-0-9992497-9-6 (soft cover)
ISBN 978-0-9989302-6-8 (hard cover)

Doodle and Peck Publishing
P.O. Box 852105
Yukon, OK 73085
(405) 354-7422
www.doodleandpeck.com

Library of Congress Cataloging in Progress #2017948578

Dedicated to my children, Grant, Neal, Jay and Meredith, and to their children, Titus, Elliott, Adeline, Ethan and Andrew. "Keep playing!"

—Anita Wadley Schlaht

For Clovis.

—Hazel Conley

When you ask me what I did today, and I say, "I just played,"
don't misunderstand.
I'm a child.
My work is play.

When I build with blocks, it's not JUST play.
I'm learning about balance and shapes.
I might be an architect someday.

When I search the bushes for bugs, it's not JUST play.
I'm learning about nature.
I may be a scientist someday.

When I rescue someone in trouble, it's not JUST play.
I'm learning to care about others.
I may be a police officer, fire fighter, or soldier someday.

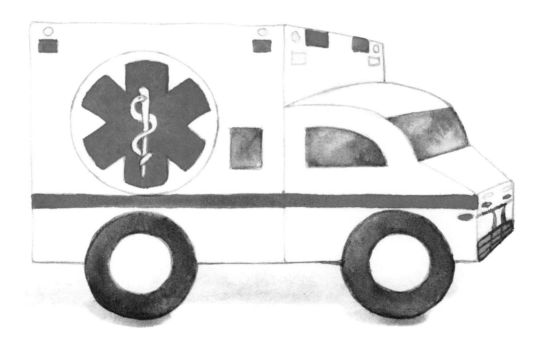

D&P

Tales

When I pretend to read, it's not JUST play.
I'm learning about books.
I may be a teacher or librarian someday.

When I help Nana cook, it feels like play.
But I'm using my senses.
I may be a chef someday.

When I lasso my pretend horse,
it's not JUST play.
I'm acting big and tough like Dad.
I may be a father and a husband
someday.

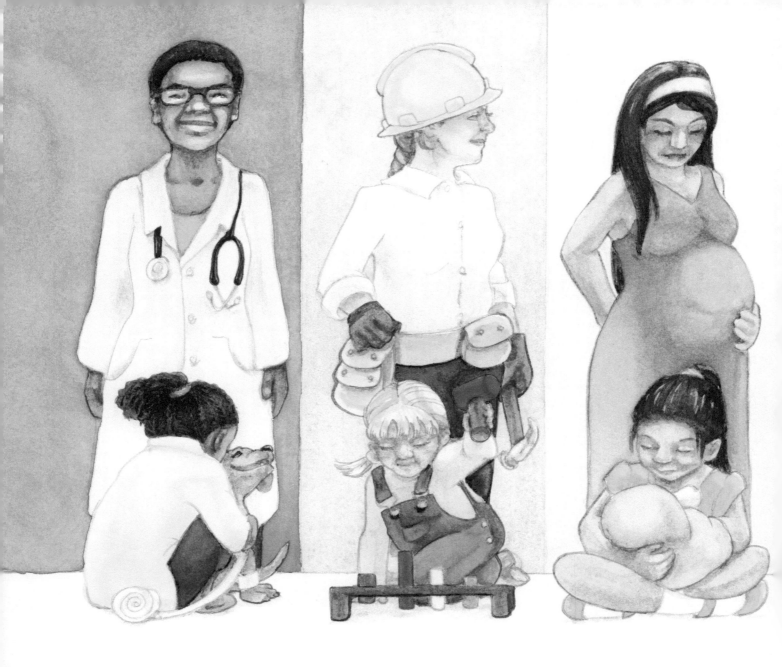

When I get big, I'll work like you.

'Til then I'll play. It's what children do.

When I sing and bang on my toy drum, it's not JUST play.

I'm learning patterns and rhythms, words and tunes.
I may be a conductor, composer, or musician someday.

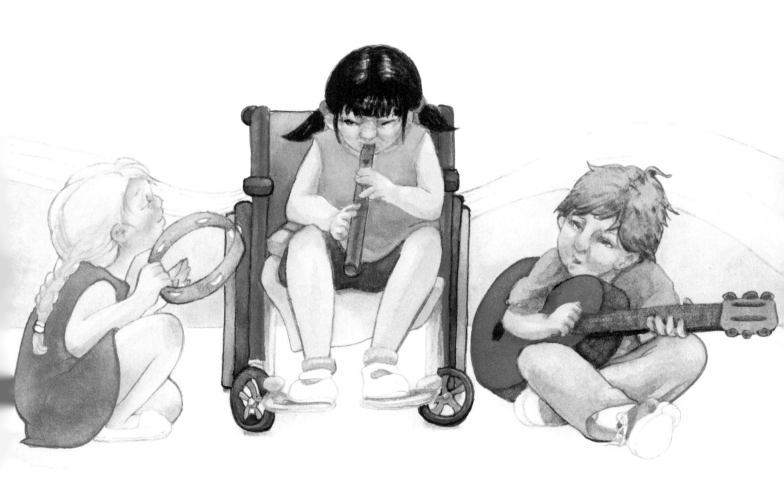

When I skip, hop, and run, it's not JUST play.

I'm learning how my body works.
I may be a doctor, nurse, or athlete someday.

When I "dress up" and care for my dolls,
it's not JUST play.
I'm part of an imaginary family.
I may be a mother and
a wife someday.

Putting a puzzle together is not JUST play.
I'm learning to solve problems.
I may be an engineer or inventor someday.

When I scribble words or tell wild tales, it's not JUST play.
I'm using my imagination.
I may be a writer someday.

When I paint, or mold and shape my clay, it's not JUST play.
I'm sharing ideas and feelings through color and shape.
I may be an artist someday.

So when you ask me what I did today,
and I answer, "I just played,"
don't misunderstand.

I am a child.
My work is play.

Anita Wadley Schlaht, Author

In 1974, as a first year preschool teacher, Anita wrote the poem **Just Playing**. It is still used to motivate teachers and parents to value the role of play in a child's life. The poem is now a children's book entitled **Just Playing**. Schlaht holds a Master's degree in Gifted Education and is currently a museum Executive Director.

Hazel Conley, Illustrator

Hazel Conley, a watercolor/pen and ink artist, earned her Bachelor of Arts from UCO and her Master of Fine Arts from SCAD. Follow Conley on both Instagram and Facebook. These links and her gallery can be found at www.dreaminghazeltudio.com

CPSIA information can be obtained
at www.ICGtesting.com
Printed in the USA
BVHW02n2319190818
524895BV00002B/10/P